Bee makes tea

Lesley Sims

Illustrated by Fred Blunt

Meet Bee.

Bee lives
beside the sea.

Today she's all a-flutter, for it's Queen Bee's birthday tea.

Bee buzzes home
and starts to bake.

Soon her rooms fill up with cake.

Chocolate cheesecakes on the chairs...

Cherry cupcakes
up the stairs...

Pies piled high with
plums and pears.

Ant runs in and grins with glee.
"You're making tea!"

For my Queen Bee.

"Her birthday tea is by the sea."

They stack up cups and fill the pot.
Bee starts to frown. It looks a lot.

"Oh Ant, how will I carry that?"
"Wait there," says Ant.

I'll soon be back.

He finds his friends and lines them up.

They carry cakes and plates and cups.

Two take the milk.
Three take the pot.

"Wow!" says Ant.
"That cake is tall."

"Speed up!" shouts Ant.
"Move that cake faster."

Then one ant slips and trips...
Disaster!

"Oh no!" Bee cries.
She sobs and sighs.

That *was* my Queen Bee's big surprise.

"The Queen will be so mad with me.
She'll say that I'm a bad, bad bee."

"Collect it all," Ant tells his team.
"Now quick, Bee!
Whip some buttercream."

"You need to use the cream like glue...
See? Stuck together, good as new."

The Queen Bee gasps and laughs,
"Hee, hee! A special cake
that looks like me?"

"Thank you for my birthday tea!"

About phonics

Phonics is a method of teaching reading used extensively in today's schools. At its heart is an emphasis on identifying the *sounds* of letters, or combinations of letters, that are then put together to make words. These sounds are known as phonemes.

Starting to read
Learning to read is an important milestone for any child. The process can begin well before children start to learn letters and put them together to read words. The sooner children can discover books and enjoy stories and language, the better they will be prepared for reading themselves, first with the help of an adult and then independently.

You can find out more about phonics on the Usborne Very First Reading website, **www.usborne.com/veryfirstreading** (US readers go to **www.veryfirstreading.com**). Click on the **Parents** tab at the top of the page, then scroll down and click on **About synthetic phonics**.

Phonemic awareness

An important early stage in pre-reading and early reading is developing phonemic awareness: that is, listening out for the sounds within words. Rhymes, rhyming stories and alliteration are excellent ways of encouraging phonemic awareness.

In this story, your child will soon identify the *ee* sound, as in **bee** and **tea** or **queen** or **team**. Look out, too, for rhymes such as **chairs** – **stairs** and **sighs** – **surprise**.

Hearing your child read

If your child is reading a story to you, don't rush to correct mistakes, but be ready to prompt or guide if he or she is struggling. Above all, do give plenty of praise and encouragement.

Edited by Jenny Tyler
Designed by Caroline Spatz

Reading consultants: Alison Kelly and Anne Washtell

First published in 2013 by Usborne Publishing Ltd., Usborne House, 83-85 Saffron Hill, London EC1N 8RT, England.
www.usborne.com Copyright © 2013 Usborne Publishing Ltd.